Disney·PIXAR
Merida

Chasing
Magic

To Mrs. Haines's fourth-grade class
at Wedgewood —S.B.Q.

With appreciation to Aki Yanagi, who always
helps us with the translation —G.

randomhousekids.com

ISBN 978-0-7364-3290-0 (hc) — ISBN 978-0-7364-8248-6 (lib. bdg.)

Printed in the United States of America

10 9 8 7 6 5 4 3 2 1

DISNEP · PIXAR

Merida

Chasing Magic

By Sudipta Bardhan-Quallen
Illustrated by Gurihiru

Random House 🏠 New York

Chapter 1

The sun had barely risen, but Castle DunBroch was already alive with activity. Only one person was still in bed.

"Merida!" The queen's voice echoed through the halls. Merida pulled her pillow over her head. Anything to try to block out the sound. Her mother could be heard from anywhere in the castle—even around corners and through stone walls.

"Merida!" The voice was getting closer.

Now Merida heard footsteps approaching. "Ach," she muttered. "It's too early."

Without warning, the blankets were ripped away.

"Merida," said Queen Elinor, "how many times have I told you that a princess rises with the sun?"

"I don't know," Merida mumbled. "I don't think human beings have discovered a number that's high enough yet."

"A princess never mumbles," her mum added.

Merida opened her eyes just enough to see her mother standing over her. There she was, hair perfectly combed. Her mouth was a tight line. She arched a single eyebrow.

"I'm sorry, Mum—" Merida began.

But Elinor simply jumped into bed next to her daughter. She pulled the blankets over them both.

"If the princess is going to loll about in bed long after the sun is in the sky," she said, "then I think the queen is allowed to join her."

Merida smiled and threw an arm over her mother.

"Did you forget what today is?" Elinor asked.

Merida's eyebrows scrunched as she tried to remember. "Someone's arriving?" she asked.

"Yes, someone is arriving!" Elinor said. "Haven't you been paying attention?"

Merida bit her lip and looked away. She hadn't been following events in the kingdom very closely. After all, the Queen of DunBroch was responsible for treaties and truces. Merida was not the queen.

"Oh, Merida!" said Mum. She reached over and cupped her daughter's chin. She lifted her face until they were eye to eye. "I know this treaty doesn't seem as interesting to you as climbing or riding or shooting at things with that bow of yours. . . ."

"It's called archery, Mum."

"I *know* it's called archery, silly goose," Elinor said. "Treaties may not seem as interesting," she continued, "but they are important. I expect you, as Princess of DunBroch, to learn from this. That way you will know what to do when you are queen yourself."

"Fine, Mum," Merida mumbled.

"Did you practice your song?" Elinor asked.

Merida pulled the blankets up higher. Mum wanted her to be ready to sing a song for the guests. But singing was one of those princess skills that Merida would never master.

Mum sighed. "You *will* practice today?"

But Merida wasn't loving the thought of getting out of bed. "Just a bit longer?"

"No lolling about, Merida," Mum said. "A princess never lolls about." But when she rose from the bed, she tucked the blankets around her daughter. "A *wee* bit more," she whispered, and then straightened her skirts and crown. "Then get dressed and come to the games field. You can practice your song there."

Elinor turned to Merida's armoire. A wimple was hanging from one corner. Merida's heart plummeted. Mum hadn't made her wear that stupid thing since the Highland Games, when she had it wrapped around Merida's head and hair like a cloth prison. But today would be the first important day since the Games. Merida should have known that a "traditional" headdress would be a part of that.

Elinor lifted the wimple and fingered the white fabric. "Merida," she said. Her eyes locked with her daughter's. Merida held her breath. "Don't wear this ridiculous thing today, please?"

The games field was buzzing with people when Merida arrived. But Mum was nowhere to be found. Merida only saw her father, King Fergus, holding court.

"Everything must go well today," Fergus bellowed. Lords Dingwall, Macintosh, and MacGuffin, who had traveled from their own lands to help with the treaty, nodded solemnly.

"Elinor will kill me if anything goes wrong!"

"And a treaty would help our people prosper," Lord Dingwall added.

Fergus grinned sheepishly. "Yes, of course—that, too." When he spotted Merida, he whispered to her, "But keeping your mum happy is even more important!"

As Merida giggled, the games field grew silent.

The lords turned and bowed. Fergus smoothed his kilt. The triplets even hid the cakes they had stolen behind their backs. Only one person could command the people of DunBroch in this way. Mum had made her entrance.

"My people," Elinor began. "This is an historic day. The Lord of Cardonagh's ships will land today to discuss a treaty between our kingdoms. If we come to an agreement, the people of DunBroch will be able to trade freely with the people of Cardonagh. This will bring prosperity."

"Aye!" cried Fergus. He crossed the field to lead Elinor up to the dais. They clasped hands and stood side by side while the people cheered for their king and queen. Merida smiled. Her parents were so happy together. Their love was the cornerstone of the kingdom.

"Just as the clans DunBroch, Macintosh, MacGuffin, and Dingwall once united," Elinor continued, "now we ally with other friends." The queen looked over to Merida and held out her hand. Merida took a deep breath and walked to the dais. She held her head up like her mother. *Princesses walk with dignity,* Mum had said so many times. Merida wanted her to know that she *did* listen. Sometimes.

As Merida approached, Elinor took her hand. "Upon signing this treaty," she said, "DunBroch and Cardonagh will be allies. The future is most precious to us. My daughter, Merida, is your princess. This treaty is for her and for all our children."

"Hear, hear!" shouted Lord Dingwall. Others began to cheer as well. Elinor held up her hand for silence.

"To honor our hopes for the future, Lord Braden is bringing a member of his family, his heir, to DunBroch."

Merida's head snapped up. An heir? She didn't remember anyone mentioning any heirs. Suddenly, she wished she *had* paid more attention to the preparations.

Merida's heart began to pound. What was her mother about to say?

"If we are successful," Elinor said, "then we will celebrate a lifelong bond between DunBroch and Cardonagh."

Lifelong bond? Merida thought her parents had given up on the idea of arranging a marriage between her and some lord's son. But an heir and a lifelong bond? Marriage might be back on the table.

No, Mum wouldn't do that, she thought. But then the crowd erupted in cheers. Elinor and Fergus grasped Merida's hands and raised them into the air in celebration. *This is lucky,* Merida thought. *If I faint, they'll be holding me up.*

As soon as the cheering died down, Merida

tried to pull Mum aside. But Elinor was busy discussing the banquet with Maudie. Merida knew that once Mum started talking about haggis, it would be a long time before she was done.

Merida sighed and looked for her father instead. But Fergus had gone to meet the ships from Cardonagh. There was no one to ask about the heir and why he was coming.

"Mum and Dad would never arrange another marriage," Merida whispered. Why did it sound like she was trying to convince herself?

Merida glanced at her mother again.

"Some people like a baked haggis," Elinor said, "but I prefer a boiled haggis." Maudie nodded solemnly.

There was no way to get any answers out of

Mum now. Merida needed some time to think.

She quietly backed away from the hulla-balloo. When she was out of sight, she ran back to the castle and to her room.

In a few minutes, she was headed toward her horse with her bow in hand.

"I need some time alone, Angus," Merida said when she reached the stable. "Let's go for a ride."

Soon Angus and Merida were flying through the Highlands. The familiar twang of the bowstring resounded as Merida fired shot after shot. When the princess was riding with a bow, she felt as free as the wind. In no time, she almost forgot about the Lord of Cardonagh.

Up ahead, hidden in the high branches of a tree, Merida spied a ripe, juicy apple. She

brought Angus to a halt. "I'll get that down for you, Angus. Won't that be yummy?"

It was a difficult shot to make, almost straight overhead. But if she hit the stem of the apple, it would fall at Angus's feet, making it easy for him to snack on.

Merida drew her bow. Before she released the string, an arrow flew toward the apple. It sliced the stem perfectly. The apple plopped to the ground.

"What was that?" Still holding her arrow in place, Merida turned to look over her shoulder.

Behind her, on horseback, was a strange girl holding a longbow.

The girl asked, "Did I take your target?"

Chapter 2

"I'm so sorry," the girl said. She jumped down from her saddle, her long black braids swinging. She scooped the apple off the ground and used the hem of her cloak to wipe it clean. "Here you go," she said, holding it out to Angus. He sniffed at the apple, then chomped it.

Merida blurted, "Crivens! What a shot!"

The girl broke into a radiant smile. "Thank you! I'm so glad you're not mad!"

"Mad?" Merida snorted. She leaped out of her saddle and joined the girl on the ground. "I want you to show me how you did that!"

The girl giggled. "Anytime."

"I'm Princess Merida of Clan DunBroch," Merida announced. Mum would expect her to show her manners. Then she giggled, too. "But you can just call me Merida."

"And I'm Catriona," the girl answered. "I go by Cat. I'm glad to meet someone who likes archery as much as I do."

Merida couldn't agree more. But before Merida could say anything else, she heard a thundering of hooves. Angus's ears pricked up and Merida readied her bow. It was clearly a large party of horses approaching. *There's no way Mum and Dad would send that many men after me,* Merida thought. *Not for leaving the games field.*

"Cat!" Merida shouted. "Quick! Mount your horse. We don't know who's coming!"

But there was no time. Within moments, riders emerged from the trees. Angus's nostrils flared. He moved closer to the girls. Merida's grip on her bow tightened.

One rider broke away from the pack and headed for Merida and Cat. He was dressed differently from the others. The rest of the men wore simple black-and-white clothes. This one wore a kilt. But Merida didn't recognize the tartan—it didn't belong to any clan she knew.

The rider shouted, "There she is!"

Merida drew her bowstring back. Cat

reached out and grabbed the bow.

"What are you doing?" Merida hissed.

"Don't shoot!" Cat cried. "He's here for me!"

"That is correct, my lady," said the rider. His voice was deep and rich. He shouted to the other riders, "Stay back! I will handle this." It was obvious that the other men took their orders from him. Not one of them moved.

"My lady," he said to Merida. "I mean you no harm." His words were reassuring, but he still gave Merida the collywobbles.

Merida took a step away. Cat grabbed her hand and pulled her forward.

"This is Princess Merida," she said.

The man dismounted and bowed. When he leaned over, Merida spied a glittering locket hanging from his neck. She couldn't explain why, but a chill ran down her spine.

Maybe the man sensed Merida's unease. He smiled and held out his hand, palm up. His other hand reached for his locket. While Merida watched him, something shimmered and glowed in his palm. Then a flower materialized out of nowhere. "For you, Princess Merida."

"Magic!" Merida whispered. She hesitated,

but Cat grabbed the flower and held it out to her. Merida forced herself to relax.

"Allow me to properly introduce myself, Princess," the rider continued. "I am Lord Padraic. I am sworn to the Lord of Cardonagh."

"Cardonagh!" Merida gasped. Now Merida *knew* she was in trouble. If everyone had arrived while she was gone, Mum would be angry!

"I have to get back!" Merida yelped. She turned to face Cat. "You didn't tell me you were from Cardonagh."

Cat shrugged. "I was just getting to that."

"Yes," Padraic said. "She is from Cardonagh. In fact, the Lord of Cardonagh sent me to ride out to locate his heir." He looked pointedly at Cat. "Your uncle will not be pleased, Lady Catriona."

Cat had the same look on her face as the triplets did when they were caught pulling one of their pranks. "I didn't mean to cause a fuss," she mumbled.

Merida was speechless—but only for a moment. "You're the heir of Cardonagh?" she asked Cat.

"Yes," said Padraic. "And if I don't bring her back safely to her uncle soon, he'll have my head."

Cat smiled weakly. But Merida's grin threatened to crack her cheeks.

"This is amazing news!" Merida laughed. "We have to get back to DunBroch! I want everyone to meet you!"

"A wonderful idea," Padraic boomed.

Merida felt another chill, but she ignored it.

"If you would lead the way, Princess Merida," said Padraic.

Within minutes, everyone was on the road back to the games field. Merida and Cat rode at the head of the party, talking the entire time.

"Mum and Dad are preparing a banquet in your honor," Merida said. "In fact, we've been planning it for weeks!"

"You have?"

"Well . . . Mum has," Merida admitted.

"I've been so nervous about coming to DunBroch," Cat said. "I thought my uncle might make me marry one of the king's sons." She blushed a bit. "I heard he has three."

"The triplets?" Merida snorted. "But they're just wee lads!"

The girls laughed.

"I'm embarrassed to admit this," said Merida, "but I've been worried about the same thing. Because I'm definitely not ready to get married."

"Neither am I," Cat agreed.

"Why are you here with your uncle?" Merida asked. "Where are your parents?"

For the first time, Cat looked a little sad. She lowered her eyes. "My parents are gone. They died when I was still a baby. It's just me and Uncle Braden."

Merida bit her lip. How could she be such a galoot? They rode in silence for a bit.

Then Cat asked, "What are your brothers like?"

"Ach!" Merida snorted. "They're a right handful. Hamish, Hubert, and Harris. Wee devils, they are. They get away with murder. I can never get away with anything."

"Me neither," Cat said.

Merida chattered on about the triplets, and soon the girls were laughing again. Before long, the games field was within view.

"Finally," Padraic said. "Catriona, I see your uncle's banners. We must hurry!" He signaled for everyone to follow as he galloped down the hill. Cat and Merida lingered after dismounting.

"Look!" Merida pointed. "There's my mum!"

"She's beautiful!" Cat sighed. Merida nodded in agreement.

"Let's go. I want to introduce you to my family," Merida said. But Cat grabbed her hand.

"Wait." She unfastened the brooch on her dress. "I brought this for you as a gift of

friendship." Then she said shyly, "And I feel like we are already friends."

Merida turned the delicate brooch over in her fingers. "It is beautiful," she said. "I love it!"

"Here, let me." Cat fastened the brooch to Merida's cloak. "It's perfect."

"Yes," Merida said, thinking not just of the brooch but of her new friend. "It certainly is!"

Chapter 3

Merida's hopes had been high for the banquet. She'd thought she would be seated next to Cat so the two of them could talk and laugh while the adults discussed boring treaty stuff. As it turned out, Merida was next to Elinor, and Cat was on the opposite side of the long table, between her uncle and Padraic.

Even though the table was in a sunny clearing on the games field, somehow Padraic sat in the only seat that was cloaked in shadows.

Merida glanced over at Cat. She was playing the part of the perfect princess, eating daintily and listening intently whenever Braden or Padraic spoke to her. She was silent and well-behaved, not distracted by anything. Not even by the triplets, when they circled the table balancing a stack of sweet pies. Not even by Merida trying to catch her eye.

The banquet was the same mind-numbing affair that banquets always were.

Lord Braden barely said a word during the meal. His face was so serious, he could have been carved from stone. He seemed to be having as little fun as Merida.

At least I'm not wearing a wimple, Merida thought.

Merida wasn't sure how, but at that exact moment, Mum must have known what she was thinking. Elinor leaned over and whispered, "Your hair looks so much nicer loose, Merida. After we finish with this treaty, let's discuss outlawing wimples for good."

While Merida and Elinor shared a smile, Fergus rose and called for attention. "My lords!" he bellowed. "And ladies," he added, winking at Elinor and Merida. "As king, I want to officially welcome Lord Braden and the other representatives of Cardonagh to our home."

Across the table, Lord Braden stood and raised his cup. All the guests quieted, expecting him to give a speech. Instead, he only said,

"Thank you," and sat back down.

Fergus glanced at Elinor. He looked as if he didn't know what to do next. The lords fidgeted. Even Merida was uncomfortable in the silence.

Only Elinor seemed unruffled. She slowly stood. Fergus took the opportunity to sit down and give the floor to his wife.

"I would like to echo my husband's greetings, Lord Braden," she said, smiling. "And I'd like to invite you to tell us about *your* home. You have traveled farther to join us today than I have ever traveled. I find myself curious about Cardonagh. I would like to hear about it from the person who loves it most."

When Elinor finished speaking, Merida saw a hint of a smile on Braden's face for the first time.

He raised his cup once more.

"The queen is kind," Braden said. "Nothing would make me happier than talking about my home."

Merida was proud of her mother's ability to break the ice. But as Braden continued talking, Merida became bored again. Sometime during his description of the sheep in his homeland, Merida felt her eyelids drooping.

I can't fall asleep! Merida thought. *Mum would kill me!* She forced herself to wiggle her fingers and toes to try to stay awake. When that didn't work—and Lord Braden began describing his family's traditional methods of potato peeling—Merida started fiddling with the brooch Cat had given her. That was when she noticed Cat—with her eyes closed!

She's as bored as I am! Merida tried to swallow a laugh and ended up coughing. Cat's eyes snapped open, and finally, she met Merida's gaze. She quickly glanced up at her uncle. When she seemed sure he was engrossed in the details of the fall foliage in Cardonagh, she turned back to Merida. Then, for just a split second, she stuck out her tongue.

Now it was Merida's turn. She made sure her parents had their eyes on Braden—then stuck her tongue out at Cat.

Cat responded by crossing her eyes and curling her lip.

Merida held her napkin up to her mouth to hide a grin. She grabbed her spoon and balanced it on the tip of her nose. When she turned to show Cat, she realized that Cat wasn't the

only one looking at her. Mum was, too.

Merida bit her lip and placed the spoon back on the table. She mouthed the word *sorry* in Elinor's direction.

That was when Elinor stuck her tongue out!

This time, Merida couldn't hold back the giggles. Neither could Cat. Or the queen. Their laughter rang through the air and interrupted Lord Braden.

"Was it something I said?" Braden asked, puzzled.

"Ummm . . . ," Elinor began, completely befuddled.

Merida had never seen her mother at a loss for words. Merida rose from her seat.

"Lord Braden, your descriptions of your home gave us so much joy that we could not help letting it out," Merida said. "Thank you."

Braden broke into a real grin. "Thank you, Princess Merida," he said. "I am happy that you both are happy." The lords and ladies began to cheer.

Across the table, Cat winked at Merida.

"A princess always knows what to say," Mum whispered.

Somehow, in all the hullaballoo, Merida

noticed Padraic. Everyone else was smiling, but he looked like he'd swallowed a lemon.

Before Merida could ponder why, Fergus stood again. "It is time for the real celebration to begin!" he shouted.

The guests began to move from their chairs. Cat made a beeline across the room, and Merida waited for her new friend, grinning. But Cat approached Elinor, not Merida. In her hands was a soft blue shawl. Cat curtseyed.

"Queen Elinor, it is my pleasure to meet you. May I present this gift? The embroidery is typical of my homeland."

"How beautiful!" Elinor cried. "Thank you for this thoughtful gift." Then, turning to Merida, she added, "Merida, look at these absolutely perfect stitches!"

Merida nodded. But she could feel her teeth clenching behind her smile. Merida was terrible at sewing, as her mother knew. The last thing she needed was to be upstaged. Especially in front of Mum.

Luckily, Fergus pulled Elinor away, and Merida and Cat were left alone at last.

Merida breathed a sigh of relief. "Do you want to go for a walk?" she asked.

Cat nodded, and Merida led her toward the edge of the games field. From there they watched the others at the banquet.

"Look," Cat said, laughing. "Your mother is trying to make Padraic taste haggis!"

Merida snickered. "Better him than me!"

"What are your brothers doing?" Cat asked, pointing.

Merida strained to find the triplets in the crowd. Hamish and Hubert were carrying a trough of water. They set it down right behind Padraic. Merida saw them nod, and she knew they were signaling to Harris. "But for what?" she whispered to herself.

Then she saw it. "No!"

"What's wrong?" Cat asked.

There was nothing Merida could do but watch. Harris blew into a carnyx. The sound startled Padraic and he stepped back—landing right in the water trough.

Even from that distance, Merida could hear Fergus's laughter above all the rest.

Braden was chuckling, too. "Just a harmless prank!" he said.

But Padraic's face had darkened, and he

stomped off, dripping water in his wake. Merida felt another chill as he walked away. She shook her head and looked for Cat.

"Cat? Where did you go?" she called.

Merida saw Cat a few yards away, following something into the forest. She ran to catch up with her. Then she saw what Cat had seen. A wisp!

Merida remembered what had happened the last time she'd followed a will o' the wisp. She didn't want Cat to end up in the same kind of trouble she had when she'd accidentally turned Mum into a bear. She ran over and blocked Cat's path.

"Cat! Don't," she warned.

"What do you mean? The wisps are here to lead me to the magic! I have to follow them!"

Cat tried to peek around Merida. "Where did they go?"

Cat spotted a blue wisp between two trees in the distance and started to follow it. But this time, Merida grabbed her friend's arm.

"No!" she shouted.

Almost immediately, the wisp disappeared.

Chapter 4

Cat yanked her arm away and scowled. "Why did you do that?"

The shouting had attracted a crowd, including Padraic, still dripping from the boys' prank.

"What is going on here?" Elinor asked. She looked directly at Merida, expecting a response.

But it was Cat who answered. "I saw the wisps! When I tried to follow, Merida grabbed me, and now they're gone!"

As soon as she mentioned the wisps, Padraic and Braden started talking at once.

"The wisps?" said Braden. "They're real?"

"We must find them!" shouted Padraic. "Quick, Catriona, where did you see them last?"

Again, before Merida could object, Elinor took charge. "My lords," she said, in her most serious queenly voice. "If Cat did see the wisps, my daughter was right to advise caution."

Braden and Padraic glanced at each other. "Queen Elinor, I must tell you something," Braden said. "We came to DunBroch to sign a treaty with your kingdom. But we also traveled here in search of magic."

"Cat saw the wisps," Padraic added. "So we have not traveled here in vain."

Merida could sense an uncomfortable feeling sweep through the crowd. People began to whisper to each other.

"Magic?" Merida said.

"What are you talking about?" Elinor asked.

"We have heard stories, my queen," said Padraic. "Stories of the great magic that can be found in these lands. Men turning into beasts. The wisps can lead us to that magic."

Merida gulped. Could they have heard about what had happened to Mum?

"You must be talking about Mor'du," Fergus said. Mor'du was a rogue bear that had roamed their land for years. "*Some* did believe him to be enchanted."

"Just a legend!" Lord Dingwall said, and the other lords nodded.

"Perhaps," Padraic said. "But all legends are lessons, and they ring with truth."

Merida glanced at Elinor. She had heard that before. But Elinor's face was expressionless.

"My lands are ravaged by war," Braden continued. "If I could find this magic, no one would dare attack my lands again, and my people could live in safety and peace."

"I don't understand," Elinor said. "Even if it were true about this magic, how would it help your people?"

"We could enchant our soldiers," Padraic answered. "We could create an army of beasts!"

Fergus laughed. "Braden, be reasonable. How would you control all those beasts? How could you be sure your army wouldn't turn on you and your people?"

"And," added Elinor, "this magic you seek is not to be trifled with!"

"Queen Elinor," said Padraic, "I suppose you would know firsthand. We have heard tales that you were turned into a beast yourself."

All the chatter in the crowd hushed immediately. Merida's eyes snapped toward Mum. Elinor's anger was clear from the way she looked at Padraic. The lords all took a step backward.

"Lord Padraic," Elinor said, "I think you'd best be served to discover not magic, but manners." She turned to Braden. "It is getting late, and it is time for us all to return to Castle DunBroch. Lord Braden, if you would accompany my

husband and me, we can discuss this further."
She shot another glare at Padraic. "In private."

By the time everyone had gathered in the
Great Hall of Castle DunBroch, the celebration
was back to normal. Elinor, Fergus, and Braden
were still conferring privately. Merida could tell
by looking at Padraic that he was angry about
not being included. He seemed to be standing in

even deeper shadows than usual. His mouth was set in a tight line.

"Merida?" Cat's voice interrupted Merida's thoughts. "Can I speak to you?"

Merida turned to face Cat. "Of course!"

"I'm sorry I snapped at you out in the glen," Cat said. "I thought the wisps would be important for my people."

"I understand," Merida said. "I'm sorry I yelled at you. I was just worried."

"I hope we can still be friends," Cat said.

"Always!"

Neither girl had noticed Padraic until he spoke. "That was exciting, wasn't it?" He chuckled. "I don't think Catriona meant to make such a stir."

"No, of course not," Cat mumbled.

"I would like to make amends for my earlier behavior," he continued. "Magic can be serious, but it can also be fun." He turned to Lord Dingwall, who was standing nearby. "My lord, would you care to help me with a demonstration?"

Lord Dingwall looked confused. "What?"

Padraic took the locket from his neck. "My magic is not very powerful, but I do know a trick or two. Please, Lord Dingwall, help me with a simple trick."

"Oh, yes," Cat cried. "Padraic can do some funny things!"

By now a large circle of people was watching and urging Lord Dingwall to play along. Padraic held the locket in front of Lord Dingwall's face, and Merida watched his eyes go glassy.

"My lord, do you know what sound a chicken makes?" Padraic asked.

"It squawks," Lord Dingwall said. He was strangely emotionless.

"Well," Padraic drawled, "when I say 'michty me,' can you *show* us what a chicken says?"

There were murmurs of confusion coming from the crowd.

"What is he doing?" Merida whispered to Cat.

But Cat just smiled. "I've seen Padraic do this. It's funny. Just wait."

Padraic added, "In fact, when *anyone* says 'michty me,' can you *show* us what a chicken says?"

To Merida's surprise, Lord Dingwall nodded.

Suddenly, Padraic snapped his fingers and

pulled the locket away from Lord Dingwall. His eyes went from glassy to normal, and he blinked three times.

"Are you going to start?" he asked.

The crowd erupted into laughter.

"Start? We've already finished!" said Padraic. "Michty me!"

As soon as Padraic said those words, Lord Dingwall's eyes went blank again—and he started clucking and squawking. "BAWK, BAWK! BAWK, BAAWWK!"

Cat laughed. "See, Merida? Hilarious!"

Merida smiled weakly. As funny as it was to see Lord Dingwall clucking like a chicken, there was something about Padraic's ability to control him that didn't sit well with her.

"Do it again!" someone yelled.

Padraic looked right at Merida. "Princess, would you volunteer this time?"

"Don't worry," Cat whispered, "I won't let him embarrass you." She pushed Merida forward.

Merida felt the heat rising in her face. She didn't want Padraic to hypnotize her. But she wasn't sure how to get out of it gracefully.

Padraic held his locket in front of Merida's eyes. "Princess, when I clap my hands, would you dance a jig?"

"No," Merida snapped.

Padraic's eyes narrowed. He brought the locket even closer to Merida. She thought she saw the stone glow from the inside, and she started to feel herself relax.

Padraic asked again, "Are you sure, Princess? When I clap, don't you want to dance a jig?"

Merida gulped. She exhaled slowly. And then she said, "No."

Padraic clapped his hands anyway. Merida said, "I don't dance."

The crowd started laughing again.

"She's not as easy as Dingwall, eh?" someone shouted.

Padraic smiled in response. But the smile never reached his eyes. He didn't seem pleased that his spell didn't work on Merida. He laughed anyway. "As I said, my magic is weak. Princess Merida's will is stronger than any trick I could perform."

Before Merida could think of what to say, a shout rang out from the crowd. "The king and queen!"

Merida turned to see her parents,

accompanied by Braden, enter the Great Hall. The shawl Cat had given Elinor was draped around her shoulders.

"Attention, everyone!" Fergus announced. "I am happy to say that Braden, Elinor, and I have discussed everything—and I mean *everything*—and we find that we are in total agreement."

"Our treaty will be signed immediately!" Braden added. "Also, Queen Elinor and King Fergus have convinced me of the error of my earlier ways. We have discussed the magic that I had hoped to find. I see now how dangerous it can be. The people of Cardonagh will no longer look for magic here in DunBroch."

Applause thundered through the room— from everyone except Padraic.

Chapter 5

While everyone else was clapping, Merida kept her eyes on Padraic.

As soon as Braden made his announcements, Padraic's face contorted into a scowl. He drained his cup, then turned on his heel and left the hall.

"I'm glad my uncle and your parents worked

everything out," Cat said. "I was worried when your mother was angry over the wisps."

Merida smiled. "I'm glad, too."

"Merida!" Mum called. She gestured from the dais. "Bring Cat over here!"

Merida and Cat made their way to Elinor.

"Lord Braden told me that Cat has been practicing a song to sing at tonight's celebrations," Elinor said. She turned to Cat. "Would you like to sing for us now?"

Merida mouth hung open. "I didn't know you could sing!" she blurted. Cat just smiled.

Elinor signaled for quiet, and all eyes turned to Cat. She sang a song about an ancient king and a brave maiden. Her voice was pure and clear. Elinor watched Cat with such pleasure that Merida's heart sank with every note.

When the song was over, Merida forced herself to clap. She hated feeling so jealous—she wanted to be proud of her new friend. But then Elinor whispered, "Do you want to sing your song, too?" Merida shook her head furiously and excused herself to get a drink of water.

So she can sing. So what? Merida thought. She glanced at Mum and Cat, still chatting on the dais. When Elinor adjusted her shawl, Merida turned away again. *And she can sew better than me.* She shook her head. *But I don't care about those things. She's still fun and interesting. And she's the first girl I've met who likes the same things as me!*

Merida squared her shoulders. *I'm going to focus on the important things,* she thought. She decided to go back to the celebration and enjoy her time with Cat.

But Cat was nowhere to be found!

"Mum? Where did Cat go?"

"I think she went someplace with your brothers," Elinor replied.

"The triplets?"

Merida didn't like the thought of the triplets playing one of their pranks on Cat. *I should go find her,* she thought. *And probably save her.*

Merida's first thought was to check the kitchen. Nothing attracted the wee princes like dessert!

But even though she found a full plate of pastries, there were no triplets.

Merida wandered through the halls of Castle DunBroch looking for Cat and the boys. When she got close to the boys' bedroom, she heard a girl's voice.

"Cat?"

Merida tiptoed to the doorway. She expected to see Cat being held prisoner—not the scene she actually saw.

Cat sat in the middle of Hamish's bed with a book open in her lap. She was reading aloud while Harris sat nearby, listening intently. Hamish was helping her turn the pages. And Hubert had stolen a bouquet of flowers from the Great Hall—and was braiding the blossoms into Cat's long hair.

Merida watched in silent shock for a minute. She couldn't think of one night when her brothers had been that nice to her. The closest she'd even gotten to flowers in her hair was the time the triplets put manure in her wimple. It might have housed a dandelion or two.

She took one last look, then turned and walked away.

Merida didn't want to see the triplets or Cat. So she went to the one place she knew the triplets would never go—the great library. She settled herself behind a curtain in a window nook. She could still hear the celebrations in the hall. But she didn't want to go back. She just wanted to be alone.

Nothing was turning out the way it was supposed to. She'd thought Cat was just like her, that they'd be like two peas in a pod. Instead, Cat was turning out to be a *better* version of Merida—one that her family seemed to like *more* than the original.

When footsteps echoed through the library, Merida froze. *Not the boys,* she thought. *I don't want to be found.*

If she stayed very quiet and still, she decided, the triplets would think the library was empty and go away. But then she heard a voice—one that clearly belonged to Lord Padraic.

"There must be a book about it somewhere," he murmured. Merida peeked around the curtain. Padraic was scanning the shelves.

"The will o' the wisps are too important in this land for there to be no books about them," he continued. "Catriona was able to summon them. I need to learn their secrets!"

"She didn't summon the wisps!" Merida

blurted. She clapped her hand over her mouth. But it was too late.

"Who's there?" Padraic said.

Merida stepped forward.

Padraic scowled, but caught himself. "I'm sorry for shouting, Princess Merida. I just thought I was alone." He cocked his head. "Did you say something about the wisps, Princess?"

Merida wrung her hands. She didn't want to

tell Padraic about the wisps. But *she'd* spoken up, after all.

"I was just saying that I don't think Cat summoned the wisps. They've been appearing to me since I was a wee lass."

"So *you* summoned them?" Padraic asked.

"I don't think they get *summoned,*" Merida explained. "You just find them."

But Padraic had already turned back to the bookshelves. "You just find them," he echoed. "Maybe one must have noble blood."

Merida shook her head. She was about to ask why Padraic still wanted to find the wisps, after Braden had agreed to stop looking. But she was interrupted by her father's voice.

"Merida!" he shouted. "Where are you, lass?"

"I'm here, Dad!"

Fergus and Braden marched into the library, side by side.

"My girl!" Fergus boomed. "Lord Braden and I have made a wager. He thinks that Cat is a superior archer." Fergus paused and winked. "But I don't think there is a better archer in all the land than my beloved daughter. Will you help us settle this wager tomorrow?"

For a moment, Merida wasn't sure. Cat had hit her target perfectly this morning. But her father's confidence quickly made her hesitation fade away. Merida leaped up and wrapped her arms around Fergus in a big bear hug.

"I'd be honored to!" Merida answered.

Chapter 6

"Come on, Angus!" Merida patted her horse's nose to wake him. "I know it's early. But who could sleep on a day like this?"

Angus whinnied sleepily and closed his eyes. Merida grabbed the reins and led him out.

At the games field, Merida stood in front of an archery target. She made her first three shots easily. "Ach, that's no challenge!"

She stepped back twenty paces and prepared to shoot again. The target looked much farther away. She steadied her bow arm and pulled the arrow back against her cheek. She slowly let out her breath and prepared to loose the arrow.

"There you are!" someone shouted. The sound startled Merida, and the arrow flew off. It hit the target—at the very edge. Merida hadn't missed that badly since she was a wee lass.

Merida scowled. "Cat! What are you doing here?"

Cat smiled. "I was looking for you!" She glanced at the target. "I thought we could practice together. I suppose I surprised you. Sorry!"

Merida tried to match Cat's happiness. But the truth was she'd been hoping to get some practice on her own.

"It's just that I woke up this morning and I couldn't wait to talk to you!" Cat chattered on. "I mean, how exciting! An archery contest! Your father is brilliant!"

"I suppose," Merida said. She prepared to take the shot again. But Cat kept talking.

"And your mother! She's so beautiful. And wise. Do you think she liked my present? And your brothers really are a handful, aren't they?"

Merida grunted and tried to concentrate on the target. This time, she hit the edge of the red circle. "That was better," she mumbled.

Cat wasn't paying attention to Merida. "It must be so wonderful to have such a big and interesting family," she continued. "There's always something happening here at DunBroch! It's so quiet back at Castle Cardonagh. Uncle Braden has his meetings and discussions, but there's really no one for me to talk to."

Merida sighed. Couldn't Cat see that she was busy? That she didn't want to chat? She set up her next shot and willed herself to focus.

"Maybe I could ask Uncle Braden if I could stay on here for a while so we can get to know each other better," Cat said. "Do you think he would say yes? Do you think your parents would? Wouldn't it be wonderful if I could stay? I could be like . . . part of your family!"

Merida gritted her teeth and fired the arrow. This time, it was much closer to the center— maybe only a finger's width off.

"Michty me!" Cat shouted. "What a shot!"

Merida smiled, pleased with herself. Suddenly, she felt more gracious. "Do you want a turn?" she asked.

"Yes, of course!" Cat answered. She readied her own bow.

As Merida watched Cat set up, her fingers played with the brooch Cat had given her.

Cat barely stopped talking as she took aim. "I always wanted a sister," she said. Then she almost casually fired the arrow. "I know you're not really my sister, but if Uncle Braden lets me stay, it would be almost like that, wouldn't it?"

Merida knew that Cat was waiting for her to say something. But even though her mouth was open, nothing came out. All she could do was stare in silence at Cat's arrow.

It had hit in the dead center of the target.

"Crivens!" said Cat. "That was lucky!"

Merida couldn't take it anymore. Her hands closed into fists and her mouth curled into a snarl. "Lucky? You're always lucky, aren't you?"

Cat raised her eyebrows in shock. "What are you talking about?"

"Well," Merida shouted, "it was lucky that you're so good at embroidery—Mum loved your shawl. And it was lucky that you're so good at singing—the entire castle loved your song. And it was lucky you're so good with wee lads—the triplets couldn't get enough of you!"

"Why are you shouting?" Cat seemed genuinely confused.

Merida's head started to hurt. "I came out here to practice, Cat. Alone." She turned her back and started firing arrows again.

Cat stood there for a few moments. Then Merida heard footsteps walking away as the princess took her next shot. She was so upset that the arrow didn't even hit the target. When Merida glanced over her shoulder, she saw that Cat had moved to the farthest target and was practicing on her own. The very next arrow Cat released hit the bull's-eye.

Merida ripped the brooch Cat had given her off her dress and threw it in the grass. She knew it would only remind her of her jealousy. How could someone feel angry and sad and frustrated and jealous and overwhelmed all at the same time? She had to get out of there.

"Where are you going?" Cat called.

But Merida didn't even look back.

For the first few minutes on horseback, the only thing Merida cared about was that Angus galloped as fast as he could.

Soon they were deep in the forest. "Whoa, Angus," she said. Angus stopped in a glen and

Merida jumped to the ground.

Merida knew Angus was confused, just as she knew Cat had stood disappointed and hurt on the games field. Angus swatted her with his tail.

"Angus!" Merida tried to scowl. But her heart wasn't in it. "I did act like a brat. But . . ." She sighed. "But I just got so mad!"

Angus snorted.

"I mean, she can be better than me at singing or sewing. I don't care about that stuff. She can even be better at handling the triplets. But archery? Why does she have to be better at archery?"

Angus stepped up and nuzzled Merida's shoulder. She turned and stroked his muzzle.

"Archery is *who I am*," Merida whispered.

"Dad bragged about me! I'm going to embarrass him. I'm going to embarrass myself."

Merida felt tears sting her eyes. "What am I going to do, Angus?"

Angus neighed at the trees to the left.

"What is it?"

Merida strained to see what Angus saw. "The wisps!" she gasped. A whole trail of wisps was softly glowing in the forest.

For a moment, Merida hesitated. She had been right to warn Cat away from the wisps—they often brought trouble. She had to do *something*.

"Come on!" Merida shouted, jumping into the saddle. "Maybe this is the answer! Maybe the wisps are here to lead me to my fate!"

Merida and Angus chased the wisps all

through the Highlands. They rode past the Crone's Tooth and the ruins of the ancient kingdom, and then . . .

"Are they taking us home?" Merida wondered aloud.

She was expecting the trail of wisps to disappear within view of the gates of Castle DunBroch. But they didn't.

"No," Merida whispered. "This can't be!"

If the wisps were leading her to her fate, did the fact that they'd brought her home mean she was fated to take part in the archery competition?

Did it mean it was her fate to lose to Cat at everything?

Merida closed her eyes and hung her head. She couldn't believe it. She took a deep breath.

"You know something, Angus? It's possible to make your own fate." She urged her horse forward. "Maybe I'll still lose. But I'll not run away."

Angus whinnied his approval.

"I'm going to find my parents," Merida said. "Then I'm going back to the games field."

But when they rode through the gates of the castle, everyone was acting strange, shouting and running around. Something had happened.

Whatever it was, it was bad.

Chapter 7

"Princess Merida!" Lord Dingwall took Merida's hands and breathed a sigh of relief. "We've been searching for you. Is Catriona with you?"

"N-n-no," Merida stuttered.

"Ach," said Lord Dingwall, shaking his head, "I was hoping she'd come back safely, too. But at least you're here." He gestured to some soldiers. "Lads, I want you to watch over the princess. Keep her here safely in the castle. I'm going to join the king and queen."

"No!" Merida shouted. "I'm not staying here! What's happening?"

But Lord Dingwall had already walked away. His men took their places guarding all the doors. She was trapped in the castle.

I have to find Mum and Dad, Merida thought. How could she get away, with all those soldiers keeping watch?

I need a distraction, she thought. And who better to create one than the triplets?

"Hamish!" Merida whispered. "Harris! Hubert! Come here, lads!"

The boys scurried over to their sister.

"I need to get to Mum and Dad," she whispered. "Can you help me escape from the guards?"

The triplets looked at each other. Then they crossed their arms and stared at their sister.

"Boys! This is important!" Merida pleaded. But the triplets didn't budge. Merida sighed. "I will give you my desserts for a month if you help me. All you have to do is distract those guards over there so I can slip away."

The boys glanced at each other again. This time they nodded. They knew what to do.

They scurried off toward the soldiers standing in front of the rear door to the Great Hall, the one that led to the stables. Along the way, they swiped a plate of meat pies from a table and stuck them in Harris's pockets.

Hubert pretended that one soldier's sword was the most fascinating thing he'd ever seen, while Hamish tried on another soldier's helmet. The men smiled at the boys' antics. No one—except Merida—noticed Harris tucking meat pies into the soldiers' belts and boots.

What are they doing? Merida thought.

Harris gave his brothers a signal, and the other two waved goodbye to the soldiers. Then Harris pointed at Merida and motioned for her to move closer to the rear door.

Merida quietly got into position, pretending to study a tapestry on the wall.

Even she wasn't expecting it when Hubert and Hamish woke the castle dogs from their nap. The beasts bounded around playfully for a moment, until one caught a whiff of something.

The meat pies! Merida thought. Soon the dogs were pouncing all over the poor soldiers. One dog chomped down on a boot, trying to pull it off. Another nipped at a belt

"Ach!" a soldier shouted.

"Get them off me!" said another.

In the kerfuffle that ensued, it seemed everyone in the hall was focused on the dogs—everyone except the triplets and Merida. Hubert and Harris winked at Merida, and Hamish pointed to the door. Merida mouthed *thank you* and slipped away.

On the games field, Merida went straight for the last place she'd seen Cat: the archery targets. There, she found Fergus and Elinor conferring with Braden and the lords. She kept

out of sight, but close enough to hear what they were saying.

"This is Catriona's arrow," Braden said. "She loves these fletches."

"And that is Merida's arrow," Fergus added. "The girls were definitely here."

"Fergus, look!" Elinor shrieked. She picked up something from the ground. "Isn't this the brooch Cat gave Merida?"

"And look here!" Braden shouted, holding a scrap of yellow fabric. "This is Cat's favorite handkerchief." He grimaced as if he was in pain.

"Now, look," Fergus soothed. "All this means is that they were here, not that something has happened. Maybe the girls just went off somewhere together and lost track of time."

"They're not together," Lord Dingwall said,

approaching. "Merida arrived safe at Castle DunBroch. But Cat was not with her."

"I'm here!" Merida cried. She ran to her parents and wrapped her arms around them.

"Princess Merida!" Lord Dingwall looked confused. "I thought you were staying in the castle, where it's safe!"

"I'm sorry, Lord Dingwall," Merida said. "I misunderstood. I thought you wanted me to come show my parents that I was safe. They must have been so worried!"

"Ach," Lord Dingwall, still looking confused. "That sounds like it makes sense."

Elinor raised one eyebrow at her daughter. Merida grinned and shrugged.

"What difference does it make?" Braden barked. "My niece is still missing." He narrowed

his eyes at Merida. "You were here with her. Your brooch was on the ground, along with Cat's handkerchief. Was there a struggle? Did you do something to her?"

Merida started to shake her head, but Fergus stepped between them. "What are you accusing my daughter of?" he growled.

Braden's hand went to the hilt of his sword.

"I am not making any accusations. But until I'm sure she had nothing to do with Catriona's disappearance, I have the right to question her!"

"May I remind you that I am the King of DunBroch?" Fergus's hand went to his sword, too. "The only rights you have are the ones I give you."

"Now, now," Elinor said. She stepped between Fergus and Braden and pushed the two men away from each other. "Fighting will not help. We need to find Cat." She turned to Merida. "Can you tell us when you saw her last?"

Merida gulped. "I came out here this morning to practice for the archery competition. Cat followed me, and we . . . we took a few turns. And then . . ."

"Then what?" Braden asked.

Merida hesitated. "Then I rode away to get some air. But Cat was still here when I left!"

"You left her here?" Braden cried. "By herself?"

Merida couldn't look Braden in the eye. Was this her fault? Would Cat be missing if she hadn't stomped off?

Elinor touched her daughter's elbow. She pressed Cat's brooch into Merida's hand and then gestured with her eyes for Merida to say something to Braden.

Merida took a deep breath. "Lord Braden," she said, "the most important thing right now is that we begin searching for your niece." She turned to Fergus and the lords. "Can we form search parties? Let's find Catriona. Help me find my friend."

Chapter 8

"Mum! I want to help!"

Merida's hands were on her hips. She faced her mother with as much royal determination as she could muster. Behind her, the search parties were beginning to leave. Merida wanted to ride out with one of them.

But no one—especially Merida—could

out-royal Elinor. "You will stay here, where I know you will be safe. I'll not hear any argument about this, Merida."

Merida clenched her fists, but she didn't argue. It never made sense to argue with Mum when she was like this.

Lord Dingwall approached Elinor. "I'll lead the search to the south, Your Majesty."

"Thank you, Lord Dingwall."

When he bent over Elinor's hand to kiss it, he stumbled.

"Michty me!" Elinor cried. "Are you all right?"

Lord Dingwall's eyes glazed over, and he said, "BAWK! BAWWK!"

Padraic! Merida remembered Padraic and his magic. *His spell on Lord Dingwall must still be working. But where is he?* She looked for Braden, but

Padraic was not by his side. In fact, she couldn't see Padraic anywhere.

"Mum! Where is Lord Padraic?"

Elinor looked confused. "I don't know. Maybe he has already ridden out to search."

"Have you seen him today at all?"

Elinor scratched her head. "At breakfast, I think."

"Not since?" Merida's eyes grew wide. "He has something to do with this, I just know it!"

Elinor took Merida's face in her hands. "Merida, I know you're worried about your friend. But you can't just go off making wild accusations without any proof."

"But, Mum!"

"No buts, young lady. We have no reason to think Padraic has done anything."

Before Merida could argue further, Fergus rode up. "Elinor, I am leaving."

"Find her, Fergus," Mum said. "Braden is sick with worry."

"I will, love. You can count on me." Merida's father took her mother's hand.

Leave it to Mum and Dad to be sweet, even at a time like this. Merida turned away so she wouldn't have to watch any more of it.

That was when she saw it—a wisp! In the distance, on the horizon. There was definitely a flash of blue.

She felt a familiar uneasiness. But Merida had to admit to herself that the wisps had always led her wherever she needed to be. Even today, they'd led her back to DunBroch when she needed to go home. *Maybe the wisps can lead me to Cat.* Merida thought.

Merida looked over her shoulder. Her parents were embracing. More importantly, Elinor was not paying attention to her.

"Sorry, Mum," Merida whispered.

"Come on, Angus!" Merida spurred her horse on. They raced through the darkness of the forest. At first, they went to where Merida had seen the wisp. But when they got there, she saw nothing. "Where are they?" she whispered. "Come out, wisps. Come on out."

Angus whinnied.

They were approaching a fork in the road. Merida steered Angus to the path on the right. But as soon as they made the turn, something caught her eye.

"Look, Angus!" She pulled the reins and pointed behind them. "A wisp!"

Angus neighed. In a flash, they doubled back and took the other fork. They were finally on the right track.

A trail of wisps led Merida and Angus deeper

and deeper into the forest. *I hope this is right,* Merida thought. But she had no choice—her best hope for finding Cat was to believe that the wisps would lead her to her friend.

Suddenly, Angus reared his head and slowed his gallop. His ears pricked up and he gestured to the left.

"I hear it, too!" Merida whispered. There were voices coming from nearby, and she saw the blue flicker of a wisp. She listened closely—one of the voices, the one that was shouting, was deep and rich. "Padraic," she hissed.

The trees were too thick for Angus to go through. "Stay here and wait," Merida said. She readied her bow and followed the wisps.

Soon the voices became clearer. Padraic shouted, "You must follow them!"

Merida steeled herself and inched closer.

A blue wisp was hovering near a large rock. Merida walked to the rock and peeked out from behind it. There, in the glen, stood Padraic—*and Cat*. But there was something wrong. Cat's eyes were glassy, and she seemed to be following Padraic's commands.

"Do you see them?" Padraic shouted.

"There," Cat said, her voice flat. She pointed so slowly, it seemed that she was sleepwalking.

"What are you waiting for, lass? Go!"

Padraic's voice was so sharp that even Merida recoiled a bit. And then, for a moment, Cat's eyes seemed to clear. But Padraic held something in front of Cat's face. *The locket!*

Cat's eyes glazed over again. She started to move slowly toward the wisp in the distance.

Cat's expression reminded Merida of Lord Dingwall's when Padraic made him cluck like a chicken. *He hypnotized her!* Merida thought. *That's how he got her to go with him.*

It looked as if all the power he wielded was in his locket. *Without it,* Merida thought, *he probably has no magic of his own.*

Merida knew what to do. She readied her bow. She waited for Cat to walk a few more paces so there would be more space between her and Padraic. Then Merida took her shot.

The arrow sailed through the air and cleanly sliced though the cord Padraic was holding. He shrieked in surprise as the locket fell into the grass of the glen. As soon as it dropped, Cat blinked twice. Her eyes were clear.

It worked!

Chapter 9

"Wh-what?" Padraic stammered. "Where did that come from?"

Merida took a deep breath. Then she stepped out from behind the rock, bow at the ready.

"Let Cat go, Padraic."

Padraic stood shocked and silent. He saw

the trail of wisps retreating from the glen. "No!" he shouted, and followed the blue lights as they disappeared deeper into the forest.

Merida didn't hesitate. She ran to Cat. "Let's go!"

But when they turned to leave, Padraic stood in their path.

"You foolish girl!" he thundered. "What did you do? They're gone!"

Both girls took a step away from Padraic. Merida shuddered.

"I demand that you summon the wisps again!" Padraic shouted, glaring.

"That's not how it works!" Merida yelled. "You don't understand anything about the wisps!"

"No, *you* don't understand," Padraic hissed,

stepping closer. "You tried to trick me in the library. But I have studied the magic in your land for years. The wisps can lead me to the true source of this magic. Once I possess it, I will be able to create a beast army of my own! I can overthrow Braden and rule Cardonagh myself!"

"You manky galoot," Merida spat. "All of this has been for naught. The wisps don't lead you to *magic*. They lead you to your *fate*." Merida glanced at Cat. "They led me to her. Because it's our fate to be friends."

"You're wrong!" Padraic charged at Merida and Cat—and Cat said, "Look! The wisps!"

She pointed behind Padraic and he turned. As soon as he did, Cat grabbed Merida's hand and started to run.

"We just have to get to Angus!" Merida

cried. "Use the forest as cover!"

Merida darted into a thicket of trees and kept running. The forest was so dense, she and Cat were soon separated. She hoped that Cat was still on the right track. But when she heard Padraic's voice, Merida stopped short.

"Show yourself, Princess!" Padraic shouted. "Don't make me hurt Catriona!'

Merida hid behind a tree trunk. When she peeked around and saw Padraic, she gasped.

He had retrieved his magic locket and was holding it by the broken cord. He had cornered Cat against a tree and was using the locket's magic to encircle Cat with vines and branches. Cat was unable to move, and she looked terrified. But she shouted, "Don't listen to him! Get away from here. Get away from him!"

Padraic's response was to enchant another vine to cover Cat's mouth.

Merida gulped. She couldn't leave Cat here with Padraic! She looked around frantically for something—anything—that could save them.

That was when Merida saw the beehive hanging from a branch high above Padraic's head.

"Ach!" Merida gasped. She had a plan!

"The wisps led me to you, Cat," Merida said. "Just as they led you to me." She watched Padraic scan the foliage to find her, but she was still well hidden. "I'm not going to abandon my fate, and I'm not going to abandon you."

"Where are you, Princess?" Padraic yelled.

Using the trees for cover, Merida moved to a spot with a clear view of Padraic. Then she prepared her bow. When she stepped out into the open, she would have only one shot.

"Do you remember the day we met, Cat?" Merida called. But Cat looked as confused as Padraic. "I couldn't believe how you got Angus that apple."

Merida saw Cat's eyes dart upward—and she nodded. Merida hoped that meant Cat understood her plan.

Merida took a deep breath and stepped forward. As she did, she shot her arrow at the beehive.

Padraic saw the bow and began to direct the enchanted vines toward Merida. But it took only a moment for the arrow to zip through the air and sever the branch the beehive was on. It was only a moment more before the hive came crashing down on Padraic.

Merida heard the furious buzzing of bees over Padraic's panicked cries. He flailed his arms to shoo the bees. As Merida had hoped, he dropped his locket again. The vines and branches that had trapped Cat fell away.

"Run, Cat!" Merida shouted. But Cat already knew what to do. She scrambled toward Merida, and the two of them ran for Angus.

With Padraic's screams echoing in their ears, the girls bolted away as fast as Angus could carry them.

"Is he following us?" Merida asked. "Can you see him?"

Angus was galloping at full speed. Cat glanced over her shoulder to see if Padraic was on their tail. "No sign of him," Cat said. They were far from the sound of Padraic's shrieks.

"Then I think we're safe," Merida said. She leaned over and patted Angus's neck. "Hey, boy, you can relax. He's nowhere near us."

Angus nodded and slowed to a canter.

"How far are we from DunBroch?" Cat asked. "Everyone must be so worried!"

"Angus will get us home," Merida said, turning slightly to face Cat. "Trust me."

"Oh, Merida!" Cat sighed. "I do trust you! You saved me!" Cat was smiling, but that made Merida feel awful.

"Cat," Merida mumbled, "I am so sorry that I left you on the games field. If only I'd stayed, this never would have happened."

"No," Cat replied. "Padraic had a plan. He would've done this anyway. It isn't your fault."

Merida let out a deep whoosh of air. She hadn't realized she'd been holding her breath until right then. "So you're not mad?"

"Mad? No, I'm not mad," Cat answered. Then her eyes shifted away and she said quietly,

"But . . . why were you so mad at me?"

"I wasn't mad. I was . . . jealous."

"Jealous? Of what?"

"Jealous of you!" Merida threw her hands up. "You and your sewing and singing. And how you get along with the triplets! And if that isn't bad enough, you have to be good at archery, too?"

As soon as the words were out, Merida felt the heat creep into her face. She was blushing furiously, and she couldn't look at Cat. The last thing she expected was to hear her friend . . . laughing.

"What? What's so funny?"

"Me?" Cat snickered. "Good at sewing? And singing? Are you daft?"

Merida scratched her head. "But the shawl! And the song!"

"I bought the shawl at market before we sailed! Yes, that embroidery is a style we favor in Cardonagh—but I can't do it! And the song—I practiced that every day of the long journey here just so I wouldn't embarrass myself. It's the only song I know!"

Merida's mouth hung open. "You're not a singer? And you can't sew?"

"And your brothers?" Cat added. "Don't even start with them. I thought they were placing flowers in my braids. Do you know what they really did?"

Merida shook her head.

"They tied my braids to the bedpost! It took forever to get free!"

Merida laughed. She'd been jealous over nothing. "And how about the archery?" she asked. "Was that just good luck, too?"

"No, I'm actually really good at that," Cat said.

Merida wrinkled her nose and giggled. But then she suddenly stopped. "Do you hear that?"

Cat nodded. "Hoofbeats? Could it be Padraic?"

Merida listened hard for a moment. And then she broke into a grin. A familiar voice in the distance bellowed, "I'm going to catch that simperin' jackanapes!"

"Cat! Angus! We're safe!" Merida shouted. "That's my dad!"

Chapter 10

"Merida!" Fergus wrapped his arms around his daughter so tight, she was afraid she'd be smothered. "We were so worried about you!"

"I'm fine, Dad!" Merida protested. But she didn't pull away. For a moment, Merida let herself feel safe in her father's arms. Then before she knew it, the whole story of Cat's kidnapping and Padraic's scheme came pouring out.

When she was done, Fergus's face darkened and his hand clenched around the hilt of his sword. "Padraic will pay for this," he hissed.

Soon everyone was riding for the glen where Merida and Cat had faced Padraic.

"Look everywhere!" Fergus shouted. "I want him found."

"Aye," Braden agreed. "Padraic has much to answer for."

Men scoured the nearby woods, but there was no sign of Padraic. Merida and Cat looked around the glen.

"Do you see him?" Cat whispered.

Merida shook her head. The beehive she'd shot down lay cracked on the grass. Most of the bees had flown away, but there was still a faint buzzing in the air. She wandered closer to the hive. Then she saw something.

"Look!" Merida knelt next to a thorny bush. A piece of torn tartan was tangled in the thorns. "It's Padraic's, isn't it?"

Cat nodded. "And look there!" Cat leaned over and picked up a broken piece of cord from the grass. "Isn't this from Padraic's locket?"

"Yes, but where's the locket itself?" Merida scanned the grass. "I don't see it anywhere."

"He must have come back for it before running away," Cat said.

Merida's fingers clenched around the torn tartan. She knew Cat was right. She hated that Padraic had gotten away.

Merida and Cat showed the torn cloth and the cord to Fergus and Braden.

"My men will keep looking," Fergus said. "But I think we've seen the last of Padraic for a while."

Braden's face was grim. "I am sorry to have brought him to your kingdom, Fergus." He turned to Merida. "I apologize to you as well, Princess, for accusing you of trying to hurt my niece. I should have known better."

Cat reached out and squeezed Merida's

hand. "She saved me, Uncle Braden."

"She did," Braden said.

Merida smiled. "I know you didn't mean it, Lord Braden. You were just worried about Cat. I was, too."

"I'm glad you girls are safe," Fergus said. "Now let's go home. Elinor will be waiting for news." He winked at Merida. "And I don't like to keep my wife waiting!"

"Oh, Mum!" Merida gasped. "I snuck away when she wasn't looking. She must be so mad!"

"She will be proud of you," Cat said.

"Proud *and* mad," Fergus whispered. "We'd best be off!"

Back at Castle DunBroch, Elinor insisted on hearing every last detail from Merida and Cat. "Start with how you convinced your brothers to help you," she said.

Merida blushed and began. With Cat's help, she told Elinor everything.

"That was a dangerous and foolish thing you did," the queen said. "I had no idea where you were!" She kissed her daughter gently on the forehead. "But I am proud of you, for trusting your fate and for taking care of your friend. It was worthy of a true princess."

Merida beamed and wrapped her arms around Elinor's neck. "I love you, Mum," she whispered.

Elinor stepped back, holding one of Merida's

hands. She took Cat's hand as well. "Catriona," she said, "your uncle and I hoped that you and my daughter would form a bond of friendship that would last a lifetime. I am proud of Merida, and I am proud of you, too. You both have proven that you understand the importance of taking responsibility for each other. The future of our kingdoms is safe with the two of you."

"Are you ladies still talking?" Fergus interrupted.

"They are women," Braden added, chuckling. "Of course they are still talking."

"Michty me!" Fergus bellowed.

Merida heard a squawk nearby. Lord Dingwall was once again clucking like a chicken.

"Padraic's spell," Cat hissed. "It still has power."

"And he's still out there somewhere," Merida added.

"Do you think Padraic will return to Cardonagh?" Elinor asked.

Braden shrugged. "My lady, I do not know. I will be on the lookout. I hope you will keep careful watch over Merida as well."

"Of course," Fergus said. "That daft numpty had better not show his face here again—or I will finish what he guddled in the first place."

"For now," said Elinor, "let's forget about Padraic and enjoy our last night together before Braden and Cat return to Cardonagh."

Immediately, Merida's spirits fell. She'd always known that Cat would go home after the treaty was signed. But she still wished they could have more time.

"I hate that I'm leaving," Cat whispered, and Merida nodded.

"I will write to you!" Merida said.

"And maybe you can visit Cardonagh?"

Merida nodded. "And you can come back to DunBroch!"

The girls hugged.

Then Merida remembered something. She pulled away and riffled through her pocket. "Will you help me with this, Cat?"

She held out the brooch Cat had given her, the one she'd retrieved from the games field. "I'm so sorry I threw this away," Merida said.

Cat took the brooch out of Merida's hand. She smiled, then leaned over and attached it to her friend's dress once again.

"There," Cat said. "Perfect."

Ula Blocksage

Sudipta Bardhan-Quallen is the author of more than forty books for children, including *Duck, Duck, Moose!*; *Tyrannosaurus Wrecks!*; and *Orangutangled.* Her books have been named to the California Readers Collection, the Junior Library Guild, the Bank Street Best Children's Books of the Year Lists, and the Amelia Bloomer Book List. She lives outside Philadelphia with her family and an imaginary pony named Penny. Visit her at sudipta.com.